CLIFFORD'S CLASSICS

Stories and pictures by Norman Bridwell

SCHOLASTIC INC.

New York   Toronto   London   Auckland   Sydney

Mexico City   New Delhi   Hong Kong   Buenos Aires

Clifford the Big Red Dog, ISBN 0-590-44297-X, Copyright © 1963, 1985 by Norman Bridwell.
Clifford the Small Red Puppy, ISBN 0-590-44294-5, Copyright © 1972 by Norman Bridwell.
Clifford's Puppy Days, ISBN 0-590-44262-7, Copyright © 1989 by Norman Bridwell.
Clifford, We Love You, ISBN 0-590-43843-3, Copyright © 1991 by Norman Bridwell.
It's Clifford music and lyrics by Maureen Lee with appreciation to Don Zeitler.

12 11 10 9 8 7 6 5 4 3 2 1   4 5 6 7 8 9/0

Printed in the U.S.A.   24

This edition created exclusively for Barnes & Noble, Inc.
2004 Barnes & Noble Books
ISBN 0-7607-5884-0
First compilation printing, October 2004

CLIFFORD®
THE BIG RED DOG

For the real Emily Elizabeth

I'm Emily Elizabeth,

and I have a dog.

My dog is a big red dog.

Other kids I know have dogs, too.

Some are big dogs.

And some are red dogs.

But I have the biggest, reddest dog on our street.

This is my dog—Clifford.

We have fun together. We play games.

I throw a stick, and he
brings it back to me.

He makes mistakes sometimes.

We play hide-and-seek.

I'm a good hide-and-seek player.

I can find Clifford,
no matter where he hides.

We play camping out,

and I don't need a tent.

He can do tricks, too.

He can sit up and beg.

Oh, I know he's not perfect.

He has *some* bad habits.

He runs after cars.

He catches some of them.

He runs after cats, too.

We don't go to the zoo anymore.

He digs up flowers.

Clifford loves to chew shoes.

It's not easy to keep Clifford.

He eats and drinks a lot.

His house was a problem, too.

But he's a very good watchdog.

The bad boys don't come around anymore.

One day I gave Clifford a bath.

And I combed his hair,

and took him to the dog show.

I'd like to say Clifford won first prize.

But he didn't.

I don't care.

You can keep all your small dogs.

You can keep all your black,

white, brown, and spotted dogs.

I'll keep Clifford . . . . Wouldn't you?

CLIFFORD®
The SMALL
RED PUPPY

To Amy, Melissa, Beth, and Debbie

Hi! I'm Emily Elizabeth
and this is Clifford, my big red dog.

Yesterday my friend Martha said,
"I got my dog from a fancy pet store.
Where did you get yours?"

So I told her how I got Clifford.

When I was little I lived in the city.
I didn't have a dog.

One day the man down the hall called us.
His dog had puppies. He wanted to give me one.

One puppy was smaller than the rest.

The man said, "Don't take him. He is the runt.
He will always be small and sick."
But I loved that little puppy. He needed me.

I named my puppy Clifford.
He was so tiny that I had to feed him
with the doll's baby bottle.

We got the smallest collar we could find
for Clifford.

It was too big.

When he began to eat dog food,
we had to watch him all the time.

He was so little that he was always getting lost,
even in our small apartment.

Daddy said Clifford was just too small.
He didn't think he could live through the winter.
I was very sad.

That night I told Clifford I wished he would grow to be
a big healthy dog. I told him I loved him.

Next morning he looked bigger to me.

He seemed to have an easier time
eating his dog food.

And his collar wasn't so loose.

In fact, by the time Daddy got home
the collar was too small.

By bedtime Clifford's tiny basket
seemed a little too small for him.

So I let him sleep on my pillow again.

That was a mistake.

Next morning Mommy thought
Clifford looked different.
Daddy said, "I think he is growing."

I decided to take Clifford for a walk.
At the corner I saw a big dog coming.
I knew I should pick Clifford up
so the big dog couldn't hurt him.

I shouldn't have worried.

Clifford really was growing!
We ran home to show Mommy how big he was.

Had our apartment door grown smaller?

Daddy couldn't believe it. We put Clifford
in the garden to sleep that night.

In the morning the lady upstairs called us.
It was about Clifford.

In fact, all the neighbors
were starting to notice him.

The landlord called the police.

They came to see Clifford.

They said Clifford would have to go.

But how? He couldn't go through the door.

There was just one way to get him
out of our garden.

I was sad. I missed my little puppy.

And he missed me.

One day we got a surprise.
My uncle wanted Daddy to come work
with him in the country.
We moved right away.

Clifford was waiting for me.
I said, "Clifford, stop growing.
You are just right."

"So," I said to Martha,
"that's how I got my dog.
Tell me again how you got your dog."

Martha said, "Forget it."

CLIFFORD,®
WE LOVE YOU

To Mira and Usha McClelland

Clifford was feeling down-in-the-dumps.

I didn't know what to do.

I tried everything to cheer him up.

I served his favorite foods.
He wouldn't touch them.

He didn't even feel like playing with me.

The vet couldn't find anything wrong with
Clifford. She said he was just feeling blue.

My friend Alison thought some pretty flowers
might cheer Clifford up.

They didn't.

Clifford loves parades. The kids in the neighborhood
put on a parade for him.

He felt worse than ever. Bill and Marcia said
they would cheer him up with a puppet show.

The show was very good.
He liked it, but then...

...when the witch tried to push the girl
and boy into the oven,

Clifford got upset.

I had an idea. I decided to write a
happy song for Clifford.

I thought of words that say all the wonderful things about Clifford. I put the words to a tune.

We sang my song to Clifford.
This is how it goes...

Who's the biggest dog around?
Who's the reddest dog in town?

Emily Elizabeth loved that pup...
Loved him so that he grew up.

It's Clifford! It's Clifford!
Lovable, laughable Clifford!
It's Clifford! It's Clifford!
Good old Clifford—yeah! The Big Red Dog!

Who can be a scary ghost?
Who do children love the most?

Who takes Emily for a ride?
Who is always by her side?

It's Clifford! It's Clifford!

Lovable, laughable Clifford!

It's Clifford! It's Clifford!

Good old Clifford—yeah! The Big Red Dog!

Who waits for Emily after school?
Who takes a bath in a swimming pool?

Who tries always to be good?
Who once starred in Hollywood?

It's Clifford! It's Clifford!
Lovable, laughable Clifford!
It's Clifford! It's Clifford!
Good old Clifford—yeah! The Big Red Dog!

Who is Emily's Valentine?
Who makes every day so fine?

Every day they have a ball.
He's the best (WOOF!) dog of all.

It's Clifford! It's Clifford!
Lovable, laughable Clifford!
It's Clifford! It's Clifford!
Good old Clifford—yeah! The Big Red Dog!

The song made Clifford feel much better.
Maybe you would like to sing it, too?

IT'S CLIFFORD!

words and music by Maureen Lee

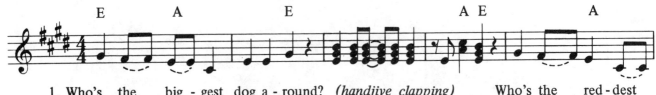

1. Who's the big-gest dog a-round? *(handjive clapping)* Who's the red-dest
2. Who can be a sca-ry ghost? Who do chil-dren
3. Who waits for Em-i-ly af-ter school? Who takes a bath in a
4. Who is Em-i-ly's Val-en-tine? Who makes ev - 'ry

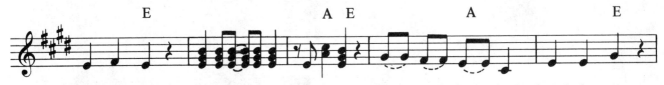

dog in town? *(handjive clapping)* Em-i-ly E-liz-a-beth loved that pup,
love the most? Who takes Em-i-ly for a ride?
swim-ming pool? Who tries al-ways to be good?
day so fine? Ev - 'ry day they have a ball!

(handjive clapping) Loved him so that he grew up. *(handjive clapping)*
Who is al-ways by her side?
Who once starred in Hol-ly wood? It's
He's the best (WOOF!) dog of all!

Clif - ford (It's Clif - ford!) Lov-a-ble, laugh-a-ble Clif - ford! It's Clif - ford! (It's

Clif - ford!) Good old Clif - ford - yeah! The Big Red Dog!
(Can be spoken.)

CLIFFORD'S
PUPPY DAYS

For Christy Jean Stalling

Hi! We are Clifford and Emily Elizabeth.
Clifford is my dog. He's pretty big.

Clifford wasn't always so big.
When he was a puppy,
he was very, very small.

I had to be careful when I played with him.

He was too small to fetch a ball.

Poor little Clifford.

He wanted to play with my toys.

They were too big.

But he liked the merry-go-round I made for him.

On cold winter days, Clifford found snuggly warm places to sleep...

...like my cap.

We put a clock by his bed at night.
The ticking seemed to lull him to sleep.

Once I forgot to turn off the alarm.

At first I gave Clifford baths in our bathtub.

He slipped off the soap one day,
and I almost lost him!

After that, I bathed him in a soup bowl.

Daddy was surprised when I told him
what I had used for Clifford's bathtub.

It was fun having such a small puppy.

But Clifford was easy to lose.

One day my aunt came to visit.

When she left, we looked all over
for our small red puppy.

My aunt found him in the bake shop.

Clifford was scared. He plopped into the cream puffs.

Then he ran through the pies.

The baker tried to catch him,
but Clifford climbed up the wedding cake...

...and landed in the whipped cream.

The baker was
a little upset.

What a mess! My aunt didn't know what to do. She didn't want to bring Clifford home looking like that.

A small boy with a big dog had an idea.
He said his dog loved whipped cream.

In no time, Clifford was all cleaned up.

I was so happy to have Clifford home again. The dog who
brought him to me was the biggest dog I had ever seen...

...until Clifford grew up.